MEGASTARS

by Michelle Smith

SCHOLASTIC INC.
New York Toronto London Auckland Sydney
Mexico City New Delhi Hong Kong Buenos Aires

To Matthew — my new reader.

PHOTO CREDITS

All photos courtesy of NBAE/Getty Images.
Cover (Dales-Schuman, Catchings), 7, 26, 28: Ron Hoskins. **Cover (Bird), 27, 32, 44:** Fernando Medina. **5:** Ray Amati. **8:** Doug Pensinger. **9, 43, 47:** David Sherman. **11, 16:** Jeff Reinking. **13, 14:** Shem Roose. **15, 35:** Kent Horner. **17:** Lisa Blumenfeld. **19, 20, 21, 22, 25:** Allen Einstein. **23, 38:** Gregg Shamus. **29:** Sam Forencich. **31, 33, 34, 39, 40, 45, 46:** Mitchell Layton. **37:** Garrett Ellwood.

If you purchased this book without a cover, you should be aware that this book is stolen property. It was reported as "unsold or destroyed" to the publisher, and neither the author nor the publisher has received any payment for this "stripped book."

No part of this publication may be reproduced, stored in a retrieval system, or transmitted in any form or by any means, electronic, mechanical, photocopying, recording, or otherwise, without written permission of the publisher. For information regarding permission, write to Scholastic Inc., Attention: Permissions Department, 557 Broadway, New York, NY 10012.

The WNBA and individual WNBA team identifications, photographs, and other content used on or in this publication are trademarks, copyrighted designs, and other forms of intellectual property of WNBA Enterprises, LLC, and may not be used, in whole or in part, without the prior written consent of WNBA Enterprises, LLC. All rights reserved.

ISBN 0-439-45602-9

Copyright © 2003 by WNBA Enterprises, LLC
All rights reserved. Published by Scholastic Inc.

SCHOLASTIC and associated logos are trademarks
and/or registered trademarks of Scholastic Inc.

12 11 10 9 8 7 6 5 4 3 2 1 3 4 5 6 7 8/0

Printed in the U.S.A.
First printing, May 2003
Book Design by Louise Bova

Contents

The WNBA is the most successful women's sports league in history.

Every year, millions of fans go to WNBA games. Millions more watch on television.

The women of the WNBA have proven that basketball is not just for boys. Girls can play ball on the playground. They can play in the gym with their friends. And now they can play in big arenas filled with cheering fans!

For the players in the WNBA, this is a dream come true. When many of the league's young stars started playing, there was no WNBA. They didn't think they could become professional basketball players when they grew up.

Now all kinds of girls can do just that! They can watch WNBA players run out onto the court and dribble and shoot and rebound, and hope someday they can be that good. Someday they will be the WNBA stars of the future!

Basketball was invented in the United States more than 100 years ago. But now it is played around the world. And WNBA players come from many different countries, including Brazil, Australia, Russia and Poland.

All of these talented, hardworking women are very different from one another. But they have one thing in common. They love the game — and they play it better than it's ever been played before!

Svetlana Abrosimova didn't grow up with basketball. She didn't watch it on television. She didn't see people playing the game on the playgrounds near her home. In fact, when she was a young girl, she had never even heard of basketball!

But now Svet, as her friends call her, is a basketball star in two countries. Part of the year she comes to the United States to play for the Minnesota Lynx of the WNBA. She is one of the team's best players.

After the WNBA season, she goes home to Russia, where she was born. She plays basketball there, too, and has also become famous there because she is so good!

Svetlana grew up in St. Petersburg, a large city in Russia. The kids in St. Petersburg loved sports. They loved hockey and soccer and ice-skating. Svetlana loved those sports, too.

One day as she sat in school, a woman walked into Svetlana's first grade classroom. The woman looked all the students over in the class and asked Svetlana to stand up.

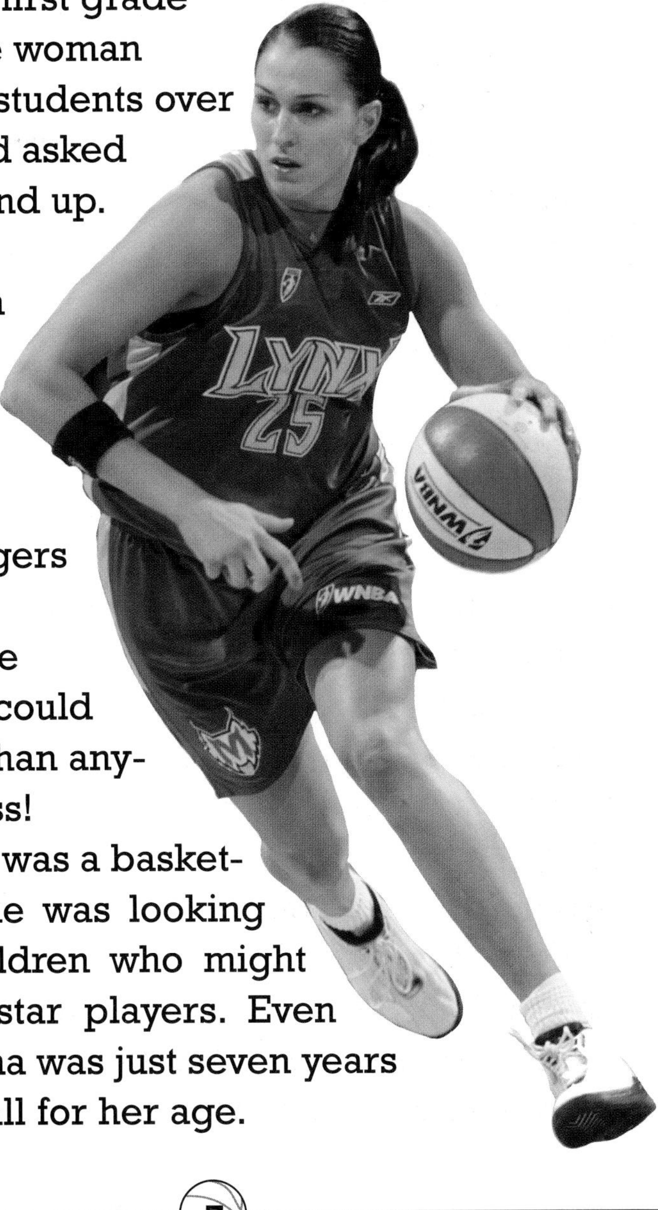

The woman asked Svetlana how high she could jump. Then she asked her to stretch her fingers as high as she could along the wall. Svetlana could reach higher than anyone in her class!

The woman was a basketball coach. She was looking for young children who might someday be star players. Even though Svetlana was just seven years old, she was tall for her age.

The coach thought she would make a good basketball player.

But Svetlana didn't know how to play. Her parents had never heard of basketball, either. But they believed this was a chance for their daughter to do something special.

Svetlana began going to a special sports school. She needed a lot of training. But she practiced very hard. When she got a chance to play, she tried her best. But she could not make baskets, and she was not as strong as the other kids.

"After the first practice, I was in love with basketball," Svetlana said. "But when I was 12, I was the last person to make my school team."

Svetlana's mother, Ludmila, decided to help. She took Svetlana to a stadium near their home after school. Svetlana would run and run and run. She stayed after practice every day and shot baskets until it was dark.

By the time she was 14 years old, she was the best player on her team!

She was so good that she was

asked to play for the Russian Junior National team. It was a group of young players from all over Russia. She would be traveling around the world to play. It was a great honor!

"I had a lot of friends who were basketball players," Svetlana said. "They were my teammates and my best friends."

Svetlana had to make a tough choice as a teenager. Her coaches in Russia wanted her to stay there. She could be a professional player and make a lot of money. Or she could go to the United States and attend college.

Her parents wanted her to go to college. She wanted to go as well. So

FUN FACT

Svetlana collects magnets in every city she visits.

FUN FACT

Svet wears size 11 shoes!

Svetlana decided to come to the United States.

Svetlana went to the University of Connecticut. The school had one of the best college teams in the country. Svetlana was very excited. But it was not easy being so far from home.

"I did not know anybody in America, and I didn't speak English very well," Svetlana said. "I did not know the culture. I had to stay up until three or four o'clock in the morning to finish my homework. It was very hard for me to handle."

But Svetlana got good grades. And she played basketball very well, too. She became her team's leading scorer, and they won a lot of games. When she was a junior, her team won the NCAA Championship!

When Svetlana was a senior, she hurt her foot during a game and had to miss the rest of the season. It was very sad because it was her last season in college.

But it was not the end of her basketball career. After college, Svetlana was drafted by the Minnesota Lynx and finally had the chance to be a pro player. But she could not play for months because of her foot. When she finally got the chance to put on a uniform and run out onto the court, she was thrilled! She was also very good. She made great passes and important baskets, and proved that she was ready to play in the WNBA.

Svetlana spends the summers playing in the WNBA and then returns to Russia to be with her family. Her mother traveled to Minnesota last year to see her daughter play for the first time since high school.

When she goes home, Svetlana spends time with her family and goes shopping with her friends. She has even learned to scuba dive in the ocean!

But basketball will always be Svet's favorite sport.

"Basketball chose me," Svetlana said. "It was up to me to stick with it. Otherwise I don't know if I would be here today."

Sue Bird

When Sue Bird was just 11 years old, she played with her girls' basketball team at halftime of a local college game.

After the game, a security guard asked her for an autograph. She wondered why he would want it. He said, "You are going to be important someday."

He was right.

Sue has become one of the best young players in the world. She is a star for the WNBA's Seattle Storm after only one season. She also helped the U.S. team win a world championship against teams from all over the globe.

Sue grew up in Syosset, New York. Her mother used to catch her climbing the tree in the backyard to see if she could watch television through the kitchen window. At six years old, she began running relay races on a track team.

Sue began playing basketball in the second grade. She wanted to play because she saw her big sister doing it. She didn't know then that she would become a pro. She only knew that she loved to play. And she would play anything.

She ran track. She played basketball. And she was the only girl on the boys' soccer team!

"There was always a team for me to play on," Sue said.

As Sue got better and better at basketball, more people started to notice her. Her family moved to Queens, New York, so that Sue could go to a high school with a strong women's basketball team.

Sue ended up at the same high school that Chamique Holdsclaw had gone to only a couple of years before. The team was used to having star players, and they had another one with Sue.

Sue was still playing

soccer and running track. But if she was going to get a college scholarship, she'd have to choose just one sport. She chose basketball.

When Sue played, it seemed like she could see the entire court. She knew when to pass to a teammate and when to shoot the ball herself. She was also a leader. When the game got close, her teammates looked to her to tell them they could win.

Everything looked perfect for Sue, but it wasn't. Her parents were getting a divorce. Sue used basketball as a way to think about something else.

FUN FACT

Sue went to the ESPY awards with Backstreet Boy Nick Carter.

Sue decided she would go to college at the University of Connecticut. She would be there with some of the best freshman players in the country. Together, she hoped, they would do great things.

Things didn't turn out quite like she'd hoped. Sue was injured in her first season at Connecticut. She stopped quickly as she was about to shoot a jump shot, and she felt her knee pop. It was a move she had done many times before. But this time she hurt her knee and had to miss the rest of the season.

Sitting on the bench was hard, but Sue did not let it make her sad. She tried to pay close attention to what the coaches and the players did during the game. It was kind of

When Sue met the president, he mispronounced her coach's name. Sue couldn't help giggling.

like going to basketball school. When Sue was finally back on the court, she knew more than ever about being a great player.

"I wouldn't change it," Sue has said. "It was probably the best thing that happened to me. I started playing like each game was my last one."

In Sue's final season, Connecticut won 39 games and lost none. Her team won the NCAA Championship, and she was voted the best college player in the United States.

Just two weeks later, Sue became the first pick in the WNBA Draft. She would play for the Seattle Storm. The Storm's coach, Lin Dunn, had many teams offering to trade their best players for the chance to pick Sue. But the coach wouldn't take any of them. She wanted Sue!

The coach made the right decision. Sue became the team's leader and one of its best players. She was an All-Star in her first season. Basketball jerseys with SUE BIRD on them sold out after just one game.

The season before Sue got there, Seattle lost more games than it won. In Sue's first season, they made it to the WNBA Playoffs.

While her team didn't win the title, they had their best season ever. And they could not have done it without Sue!

Swin Cash

Swin Cash has had a lot to live up to all her life.

When she was born, her mother and godmother picked out her name. They decided together that it should be Swintayla. Swintayla is an African word that means "astounding woman."

Astounding means "beyond belief." And many of the things that have happened in Swin's life so far truly have been beyond belief.

After just one season, she is already a basketball star in the WNBA, playing for the Detroit Shock. She has been around the world. She has been a national champion. She has even met the president of the United States!

She has her mother to thank for all of it. Her mom, Cynthia, started teaching Swin to play basketball when she was just four years old. Swin and her mother are very close. Swin calls her mother her best friend.

Cynthia was a high school basketball star when Swin was born. She was forced to stop playing in order to raise her daughter. Cynthia often worked at more than one job to support her daughter, and when Swin was a little girl, she missed her mother a lot.

"Sometimes I wouldn't see her before I went to sleep at night," Swin said. "She felt like she had to be my mom and dad, that she had to give me everything."

Cynthia wanted Swin to play basketball, too. Swin was only seven years old when she first stepped onto the playground court in McKeesport, Pennsylvania. She was one of the smallest kids on the court, but she tried hard to show she belonged.

"I tried to be tough," Swin said. "I was always pushing people down, trying to prove myself."

Sometimes the other kids pushed back. But Swin didn't quit. She was 11 when she got to play on her first team at the Boys' and Girls' Club. Her mom was the coach!

FUN FACT

Swin listens to gospel music before every game.

By that time, Swin was interested in other things, like baseball, gymnastics and cheerleading.

"The only reason I started cheerleading was because I wanted to play football and my mom wouldn't let me," Swin said.

But as she began to grow taller and taller, basketball seemed like the perfect sport for her. She was full of energy, always ready to dive on the floor for the ball or grab the big rebound.

In high school, Swin began wearing No. 32 on her jersey. It

was the same number her mother wore when *she* played for the same high school team. Then Swin earned the opportunity her mother never had — to play college basketball.

Swin moved from Pennsylvania to the University of Connecticut, one of the top teams in the country. She was joined by a group of great young players. Together they did amazing things, winning almost every game they played!

But it was not always easy. During Swin's first season at Connecticut, she hurt her leg and couldn't play. She had never been hurt before, and it was hard for her to sit on the bench and watch her teammates play.

Once Swin was back on the court,

things still didn't go right. In one game, Swin shot the ball at the wrong basket. She was so embarrassed! But she was also able to laugh at her mistake.

FUN FACT

Swin has a bobble-head doll made in her honor.

There were many better moments to come. Swin's team won two NCAA Championships. In her last year of college, Connecticut went the whole season without losing a game!

But being a pro was much different than being a college champion.

Swin's first year in the WNBA didn't start off so well. Her Detroit team lost their first 13 games. Swin had not lost this many games in four years at

Connecticut. There were nights when she just sat in front of her locker and wondered what to do. Then she would call her mother.

Cynthia told Swin to do what she did best. So she did. She played hard and proved how tough she was. Her team finished with nine wins and 23 losses.

"It wasn't normal for me, and I didn't want to make it normal," Swin said. "I just keep trying to fight against it. I tell myself that even when I lose, I am learning something."

Swin doesn't like losing, and this season she will play harder than ever. As she says, "Tough people are made for tough times."

Basketball must be in Tamika Catchings's blood. Her father, Harvey Catchings, played in the NBA. Her sister, Tauja, was a college basketball star. And now Tamika has her own basketball career as an All-Star forward for the Indiana Fever in the WNBA.

When Tamika and Tauja were young, they would go to watch their dad's basketball practice. They sat in the stands at his games. They never got tired of it! Most kids wanted to be like Michael Jordan. Tamika wanted to be like her dad.

"I loved the game from the minute I was born," Tamika said. "I can't remember a time I didn't want to be in the gym or that I got sick of shooting baskets."

Tamika was always looking for someone to

play with in her neighborhood. After a while, the boys would call *her* if they were going to play.

FUN FACT

Tamika likes to watch Christmas movies all year long.

Tamika and Tauja played in their first game when Tamika was in the third grade. Their father was the coach. And, of course, they won!

The two girls often played against each other. Some of those games got rough because neither one of them wanted to lose. They would come back into the house with bruises and bloody noses. One night, their father decided they shouldn't play against each other anymore. Tauja went up to her room.

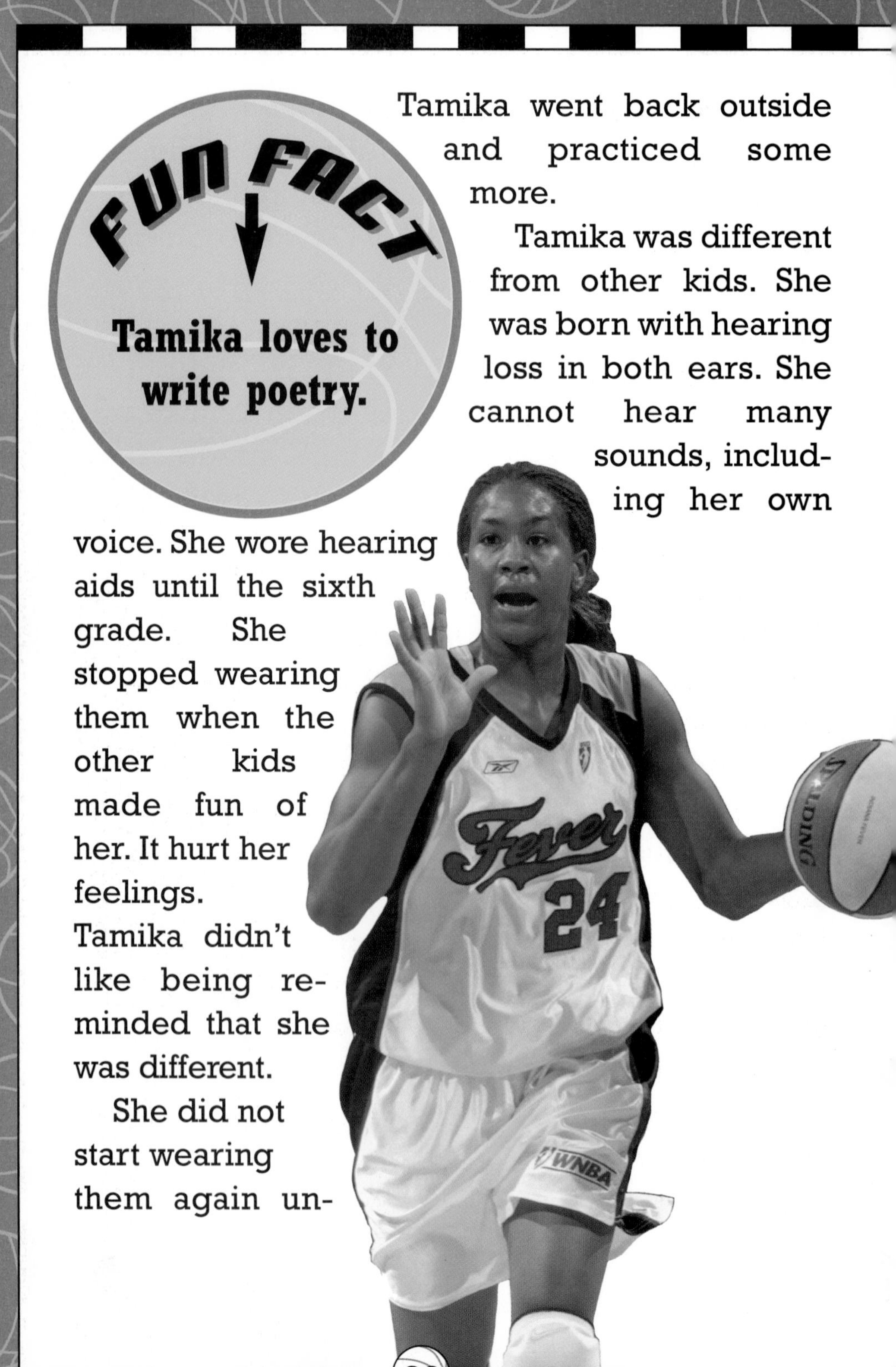

Tamika went back outside and practiced some more.

Tamika was different from other kids. She was born with hearing loss in both ears. She cannot hear many sounds, including her own voice. She wore hearing aids until the sixth grade. She stopped wearing them when the other kids made fun of her. It hurt her feelings. Tamika didn't like being reminded that she was different.

She did not start wearing them again until her college coach encouraged her to.

"She told me that if I wanted to be successful, I'd have to wear it. I do still feel self-conscious," Tamika said. "But it's only going to help me."

Tamika had a hard time as a teenager. Her parents got a divorce when she was in the seventh grade. A few years later, Tamika and her mother moved to Texas. Tauja stayed behind in Illinois with their father to finish high school.

For the first time in their lives, the sisters were apart. Tamika missed Tauja very much. They talked on the phone every night. Whenever Tamika was feeling sad or lonely, she grabbed a ball and went to the gym. Basketball always made her feel better.

Both sisters were good enough to earn basketball scholarships to college. Tamika chose to attend the University of Tennessee, while Tauja played at the University of Illinois.

Tamika was one of the best college players in the country. She won national titles in her first two college seasons. As a senior, she was preparing to try for another NCAA Championship. But she injured her knee just weeks before the beginning of the tournament. She missed the rest of her last college season.

She also missed her first season in the WNBA. Tamika really wanted her knee to get better. But instead, it got worse. She injured her knee a second time just as it was starting to heal.

Tamika sat on the bus that night, hoping that none of her teammates would see her cry. She was in a new city, Indianapolis, sitting on the bench instead of playing. She did not feel like she was part of the team.

As her knee began to heal, Tamika worked harder than ever. When she finally got her chance to play for the Indiana Fever, she was more than ready. She was great! Tamika became the team's leading scorer and was named to the 2002 WNBA All-Star team. She helped her team make its first trip to the play-offs. She was voted the WNBA Rookie of the Year.

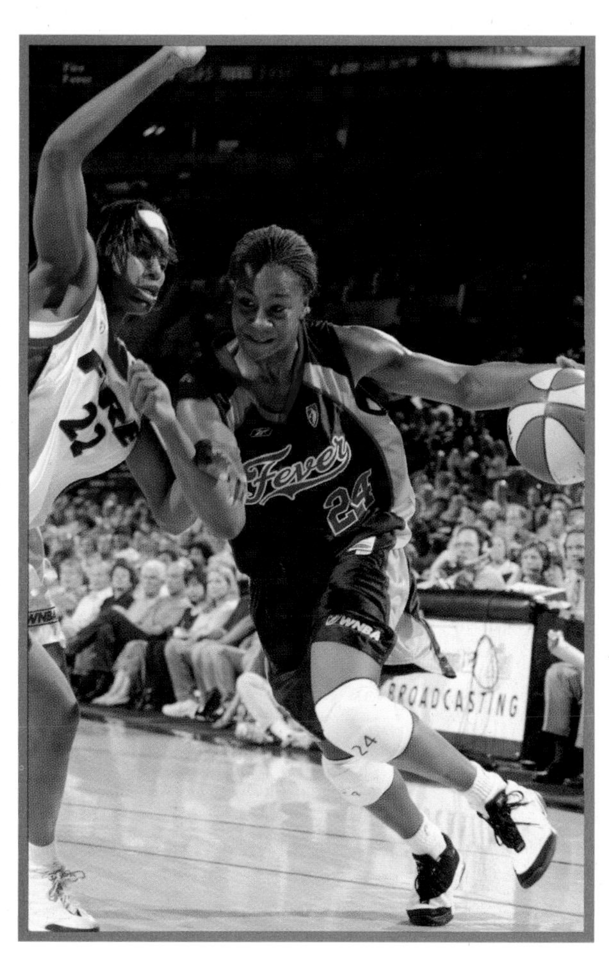

"I just want to win a championship," said Tamika. "I don't worry about awards."

But there are obviously many more awards on the way.

Stacey Dales-Schuman grew up in a hockey town. But now the people who live there love basketball almost as much.

Stacey's hometown is Brockville, Ontario, in Canada. Hockey is Canada's number one sport. Almost every kid has a hockey stick and a pair of skates.

But when Stacey plays, Brockville follows basketball, too. People gather around in restaurants to watch her play on television. When Stacey was in college in Oklahoma, they would sometimes stay up past midnight to watch her games.

Now that Stacey plays for the Washington Mystics of the WNBA, nobody has to stay up quite that late. Instead, they can watch her on television as she becomes one of the league's brightest young stars.

The first sport Stacey ever played was, of course, hockey. One day she followed her big brother, Burke, out to play. They lived in a neighborhood that was filled with boys, but not very many girls.

"My brother and all his buddies would play road hockey," Stacey said. "I wanted to play, so they made me play goalie because no one else wanted to do it."

She went home that day with bumps and bruises and scrapes. And she didn't care. Stacey loved all kinds of sports — track, volleyball and soccer. Her parents signed her up for everything. She played happily.

Stacey enjoyed basketball most of all because it made her feel creative. She could make a great pass, dribble past a defender or shoot a jump shot. It was more fun than she'd ever had. She spent hours and hours in her driveway at home practicing. She stayed late after practice to shoot baskets long after her teammates had gone home for dinner.

Stacey was becoming a great basketball player in Canada. In high school, she traveled down to the United States to play in camps with American players. She dreamed of a scholarship to a U.S. college. They did not give basketball scholarships in Canada. But not many American coaches came up to Canada to see her play.

Then one day, an assistant coach from the University of Oklahoma was on her way to the airport when she thought she would make one more stop. She came into the gym where Stacey was playing. She was very impressed. The assistant coach called back to Oklahoma and told the head coach that they should ask Stacey to come to Oklahoma.

Stacey's brother plays for the NFL.

Even though Oklahoma did not have a very good team, Stacey said yes. Being in Oklahoma reminded her of home. The people were friendly, and in the winter the weather was cold.

Unfortunately, when she got to Oklahoma, everything seemed to go wrong. At first, she was homesick. Then, just one minute into her first game, she injured her knee. She had to miss her freshman season.

Stacey's hometown is so proud of her that they have created Stacey Dales Day in her honor.

"I wanted to dig myself a hole and hide," Stacey said. "I called home every night, and my mom came down to stay with me."

But instead of being sad, Stacey decided to make her time on the bench a good experience.

"It was a great thing," Stacey said. "I was able to become a player by sitting and watching. I was able to learn."

She came back the next season and led her team in scoring.

Two years later, 20-year-old Stacey became the youngest player on the Canadian Olympic basketball team. The team played in Sydney, Australia. Even though they did not win many games,

Stacey loved every minute of it! She met athletes from other countries on the bus. She marched in the opening ceremonies. She toured a new country.

And she became a better basketball player. Stacey returned to Oklahoma more determined than ever. Oklahoma got better and better, and by the time Stacey was a senior, her team was playing for the NCAA Championship. They didn't win, and Stacey was disappointed. But not for long.

Two weeks after the national championship game, Stacey married her boyfriend, Chris Schuman. Six days after that, Stacey was drafted into the WNBA by the Washington Mystics.

Stacey and Chris and their two dogs, Allie and Gracie, moved to Washington, D.C. Chris comes to all her games and cheers her on. Last season, she helped lead the Mystics to the WNBA playoffs. It took a lot of hard work.

"I didn't really have any time off, so I was very tired," Stacey said. "But you have to get tough to get through it."

It's been many years since Chamique Holdsclaw played basketball using a coat hanger and a pair of sweat socks in the hallway of her grandmother's home. And in those years, she's come a long way.

Chamique is one of the greatest women's basketball stars in the world. She has won NCAA Championships and an Olympic gold medal. Kids wear basketball jerseys with her name on them. People stop her in the mall asking for autographs.

Chamique might be famous and talented. But she has gone through tough times as well.

Chamique was 11 years old when she went to live with her grandmother, June. Her parents were getting divorced, and her family thought it was best that Chamique and her younger brother, Davon, move in with their grandmother.

Her grandmother was tough. She made rules, and Chamique followed them. She made sure Chamique finished her homework, and that she was always polite. If Chamique was out on the basketball court too long, June would shout out of the kitchen window of her apartment. Chamique knew it was time to get back!

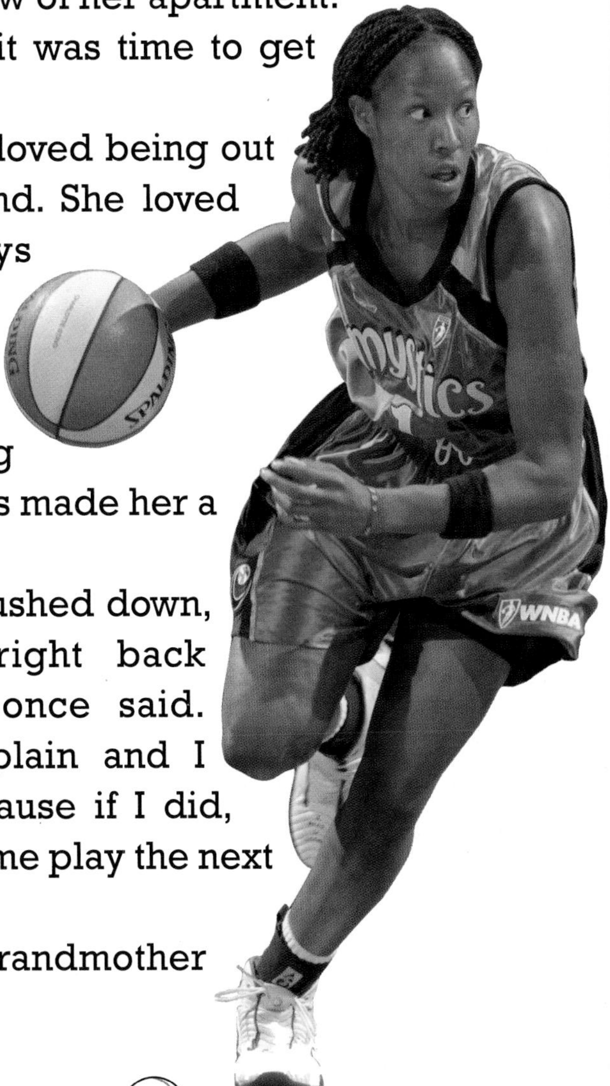

But Chamique loved being out on that playground. She loved that older boys from all over the neighborhood knew she was good. And playing against those boys made her a better player.

"When I got pushed down, I had to get right back up," Chamique once said. "I couldn't complain and I couldn't cry, because if I did, they wouldn't let me play the next day."

Chamique's grandmother

helped her to get on her first team. It was an all-boys team. Chamique tried her best to fit in. The first season, the boys did not want a girl on their team. But by the second season, Chamique was the team's best player!

Chamique has a street named after her in Tennessee.

She played every day. She would practice as much as six hours a day, coming right home from school and going straight to the court. Chamique played in all kinds of weather. If it snowed, she shoveled the court herself. One Sunday, Chamique even skipped church to play in a game. Her grandmother grounded her for two weeks.

All of Chamique's hard work paid off. In high school, her team finished every season with a championship. Chamique was offered scholarships by colleges all around the country.

She chose the University of Tennessee because she wanted to play for Pat Summitt, the Tennessee coach. Coach Summitt had a reputation for being tough and for getting the best out of her players.

Chamique was not sure she could handle it. The first weeks of practice were hard. She ran so much she felt sick to her stomach. She felt as if she could not do anything right. She called her grandmother and told her she might want to come home.

June said no. She told her granddaughter to keep working hard, and everything would be fine. It turned out better than fine!

Chamique was a star from the start. She was the team's best player. And they were the best team in the country. She made moves on the court that many people had never seen a woman do before.

By the time her college career was over, Chamique had won three NCAA

Championships. She had been on magazine covers. She was one of the most famous female athletes in the United States.

Chamique was the first pick of the 1999 WNBA Draft. She was taken by the Washington Mystics. The Mystics were a very popular team. They drew big crowds, and the fans were very enthusiastic. But the Mystics did not win as many games as Chamique had hoped. It was difficult to be on a losing team after winning so many games in college.

It took two years for things to get better. The 2002 season was Chamique's best WNBA season yet. For the first time, her team was in first place. She was leading them to victory almost every night!

Then Chamique got some sad news. Her grandmother had died. Chamique went back to New York to be with her family. After a few days, she returned.

FUN FACT

Chamique has her own brand of shoe, called BBMique Shox.

She was sad, but it did not stop her from playing her best.

"It's been kind of tough," Chamique said after she returned to Washington. "She raised me to be a great person and a giver. The best I can do now is do what she taught me."

Chamique led Washington to the playoffs. And while the Mystics did not win the WNBA title, it was the team's best season ever! Chamique had become a WNBA star. And like always, she worked hard to get there — just like her grandmother taught her.

Kelly and Coco Miller

Kelly and Coco Miller are more than twin sisters; they are best friends!

They do everything together. They like the same restaurants and the same movies. They share their CDs and their clothes. And they are both WNBA stars.

Kelly Miller
Height: 5-9
Weight: 144
Position: Guard

Coco Miller
Height: 5-9
Weight: 140
Position: Guard

Kelly is a point guard for the WNBA's Charlotte Sting. Coco, whose real name is Colleen, plays guard for the Washington Mystics. For the first time in their lives, they do not live in the same place. They do not pass the ball to each other. But Kelly and Coco are still very close.

"We talk to each other every day," Kelly said. "Our cell phone bills are very high."

Before they became professional basketball players, Kelly and Coco were hardly ever apart. They played together as kids. They shared a bedroom and were in the same classes at school. They played on the same teams from the time they were young girls.

In fact, they fell in love with basketball together. Their older brother, Kerry, played in high school. Kelly and Coco used to go to his games with their parents. At half- time, the five-year-old girls would take their small basketball down to the court and shoot baskets.

FUN FACT

Coco ties her shoes three times before each game.

"We weren't like normal kids, crawling all over the bleachers and not watching the game," Coco said. "We watched everything. We loved it."

Kelly and Coco grew up in Rochester, Minnesota. They have two older sisters and one older brother. But no one in the family loved sports as much as the twins.

They played soccer, softball and tennis. They tried golf, track, swimming and ice-skating. But nothing was as much fun as basketball.

For a long time, there was no team for them to play for. Instead, they played in the driveway with their big brother, two against one. Sometimes they even played in the snow.

In fifth grade, the girls finally got to play on a real team. And they were the best players. Kelly and Coco helped their team win their first game 67–10!

By the time they were 12 years old, they began to get letters from colleges. They did not know where they wanted to go, but they always knew they would go to the same school.

"We wanted to stay together," Kelly said. "That was very important to us."

Kelly and Coco love being twins. They are identical twins, which means they look almost exactly alike. A lot of people have trouble telling them apart. Once, they switched uniforms so their coach would not know which girl was which. Another time, they moved their desks at school to play a joke on the class.

In high school, they

were the stars of the basketball team. Kelly and Coco even shared the award for Player of the Year. It seemed as if they scored almost exactly the same number of points in every game.

Kelly and Coco decided they would attend the University of Georgia. It would be far from home, but they would have each other. The only time they spent any nights apart in college was when Kelly went away to a basketball camp for four days.

Kelly and Coco became two of the best college players in the country. Both were guards. Both could score a lot of points. Because of them, Georgia won a lot of games.

But they knew they would not be together in the WNBA.

Kelly was headed for Charlotte, and Coco would go to Washington. They would have to live on their own. And every once in a while they would have to play against each other. They didn't like that at all.

When they were kids, they played tennis against each other in tournaments. They could not wait for it to be over. When they played one-on-one basketball at home, they never kept score.

"I always want Kelly to do well," Coco said. "I don't look forward to those games at all."

Coco and Kelly had a hard time their first year in the WNBA. It was a big change.

"We were in a new situation and it was a first time apart," Coco said. "It was difficult."

But by the time their second year started, each of

them improved a lot. Both players helped their team make it to the playoffs. That was the great part.

The not-so-great part was that they had to play each other. Both of them tried not to think about it during the game. And after the game was over, they went out to dinner.

Together as always.

FUN FACT

Kelly and Coco are both huge *NSYNC fans.